DOORWAYS TO
Enchantment

POETRY

MARY W. JENSEN

Briarbook Lane Press

DOORWAYS TO ENCHANTMENT by Mary W. Jensen

Published by Briarbook Lane Press

https://www.briarbooklane.com/

Copyright © 2025 by Mary W. Jensen

Cover design by James at GoOnWrite.com

All rights reserved.

No portion of this book may be reproduced in any form without written permission from the publisher or author, except as permitted by U.S. copyright law.

ISBN: 978-1-7376437-2-2

https://marywjensen.com/

https://www.briarbooklane.com/mary-w-jensen-newsletter

Contents

Introduction

You walk through a dense forest.
You left the path some time ago,
but you do not feel lost.
Something guides you, quiet and sure,
drawing you forward.
The hush between the trees hums with secret magic.

At last, the forest parts,
revealing a clearing bathed in golden light,
wildflowers spilling over
like stars scattered on earth.
In the center stands a doorway,
its frame entwined with vines
and flickering fairy lights.

The door creaks open, silent yet beckoning.
If you choose to step through,
you will see the world with new eyes.
And once you cross the threshold...
there is no turning back.

Door One: The Mortal World

Where stories begin and wonder first stirs.

Here, in quiet places and common days,
magic whispers on the wind.
You'll find it in a glance,
in the hush before a storm,
in the ache of longing for something more.

This is the world you know,
but look closer —
the veil shimmers,
and something waits beyond the edges.
Step through.
See what you've missed.

The Child's Gift

Mama, can you smell?
my teddy bathed in wildflowers

Mama, can you hear?
this rock has a heartbeat

Mama, can you feel?
the flap of dragon wings

Mama, can you see?
the fairy sitting in the tree

Mama, can you taste?
there's magic in my lemonade

Mama, did you know?
an angel watches over me

How to Catch a Fairy

Fairies like a place to frolic —
explore a forest glade,
find a playful willow,
or circle of shrooms.

Fairies love gifts —
entice them with
a trail of flowers,
berries and sparkly things.

Fairies want to dance —
like a pied piper,
lure them with a spritely tune
played on harp, flute, fiddle.

Fairies need a home —
provide a roof made for doll or bird,
or create one just for them,
and their loyalty is yours alone.

Defending the Keep

A wall was built in defense —
four walls enclosing a sand keep,
separating the king's knights
from the army men.

It took all morning for the young god
to complete the wall —
polished river pebbles sealed by glue:
five inches high, three inches wide,
each of the four sides measuring two feet long;
only the west wall incomplete in its height,
as the god was called away from his work.

Noon sun glints off pink and gray surfaces;
the east side belongs to Egg —
placed as a watchman;
with painted face he looks back
into the shadows of his wall
at the knights positioned for any breach;
a noise draws his attention forward into the garden
where the enemy resides —
a spurt... and water sprays from the ground,
making the smooth surface slick.

Egg dares not move until the barrage ends,
but the assault has just begun —
a large furry intruder stalks,
whiskers twitching as she sniffs the musty stone...
with a swipe she topples Egg —
his wire legs find no purchase on the wet wall,
he falls to crack upon the soldiers below;
the knights can do nothing to repair him,
only mourn his demise beneath the wall.

The Unsolvable Variable

Voices drone around me.
Equations drip from the blackboard;
numbers sizzle into puddles of data.
Letters—once unknown values—
dance away to reform
into glorious words.

Words stretch and morph
into dragons,
which fly me away
from this dull room.

Time Stands Still

Time does not exist here
in this pocket of space
between willow tree and fence —
the leafy curtain separates
two different worlds:

Out there I have duties,
a proper way to behave.

In here I can act however I please —
free to be a child,
or princess or warrior,
have tea with my teddy
or read that "foolish fantasy."

Time stands still,
in my personal Neverland.

The Key's Mystery

The key itself is simple:
rusted iron on woven cord;
without its lock
it is nothing.

It may open a chest
left hidden by pirates,
or unlock a gate
to an alien world;

Perhaps it locks
a mermaid's diary,
or the chains that bind
a wolf at full moon;

It could be the key
to a dungeon cell,
or the way to unlock
a damsel's heart;

Most likely it matches
a plain house door...
but until the lock is found,
it holds everything.

Escape

A different place
A different time
A world of magic
A world of rhyme

Where flowers sing
And trees can walk
Where statues dance
And animals talk

This is the land
Of fantasy
It lies beyond
Reality

A distant place
That I can go
To find myself
And then I'd know

The truth of life
And all its quirks
For there we see
What truly works

We all have faults
Even in Tales
But good still wins
And evil fails

Sanctuary

The world can be a crazy place,
big crowds become ordinary
make me crave some breathing space
to sit beneath my willow tree.

Weather won't stop me coming here,
the brisk air of February
means many layers of cashmere
to sit beneath my willow tree.

Don't think me lonely under here,
my daydreams are legendary;
dragons, fairies, and elves appear
to sit beneath my willow tree.

If you're ever feeling slighted,
and in need of sanctuary,
know you are always invited
to sit beneath my willow tree.

Today's Tales

Today, Little Red Riding Hood would fear no wolves.
Hansel and Gretel, no witch in the woods.
Man is the monster in modern tales —
the faceless creature feeding our fears.
It's Jasons and Freddies, strangers on the street —
no magic spell or dragon's breath,
just greed, anger, mischief, lust.
Man's selfishness has banished
the magic and mystery.

The Unknown

We've pushed back the boundary of the woods,
surrounded ourselves with plastic, steel, stone —
no longer surrounded by a world unknown.
All that is left is...
...deep in the Amazon
...deep in the ocean
...deep in outer space
but slowly those too are invaded, catalogued,
leaving nothing left for imagination —
little hope for escaping our consuming civilization.

Door Two: The Hero's Path

Where courage opens the way, and every step shapes a story.

The call has sounded.
A choice must be made.
Will you go?
Here walk those who dare,
who gather hope in one hand
and steel in the other.

Beyond this door,
trials and triumphs await —
not for gods or kings,
but for those brave enough to answer.
This is the path of heroes.
Take your first step.

Hero's Journey

A magical quest
journey for the talisman
a clichéd hero

Dreams of Fantasy

The castle high
The dungeon low
To the world of fantasy
I would like to go

To see the dragons
Hear them roar
Feel their fire–breath
And with them soar

Swim with the mermaids
To the depths of the sea
Exploring Atlantis
That's where I wish to be

Or perhaps ride a unicorn
A creature of lore
To the ends of the earth
I'd never want more

But to find a white knight
One just for me
Who'd reveal my fair maiden
And set her free

To the stars above
To the canyons below
My white knight would take me
Where I want to go

Window

I lean out,
fingertips tingle as they stretch —
almost touch — clouds,
I can nearly taste the rain
from the horizon's storm.

A breeze livens this barren room —
curtains billow,
bed canopy dances,
ripples form in tainted basin water.

Rusted leaves flutter
across a whitewashed floor —
a wayward petal
still perfume-rich
settles on the windowsill.

Wind whispers
telling tales of freedom
and of you
(whoever you are)
looking for me.

If I did not believe its truth
I would throw myself
to kiss the earth never touched,
or wrap a noose of curséd hair
around my pale neck.

I will wait
a bit longer.
I will not live another winter
alone
in this weathered tower.

Sleeping Beauty

In her tall tower
She lies on pillow still pristine;
Castle trapped in time.

Poisoned dreams
Curl like vines around her mind,
Imprison her in slumber.

Try to wake her with a kiss.
Is she still sleeping?
Silence.

Your fight through thorn and bramble
All for naught —
She awaits another.

"If it smells like a trap, it probably is one."

Always by your side
your best friend
I test the trail ahead
push and tug to guide you.

You laugh at my antics
call me playful, a tease
and trod on
only to find a dead end

Or worse, a netted trap
as bandits ambush
and dragons come to feed.

Why bring me along
if you ignore my instincts
every time?

Trust my nose
trust my bark
find another path
don't walk into
another trap.

Sparky's Magic Shop

Is your boss a big buffoon?
We can make him a baboon!
Homework making you insane?
We can biggify your brain.

We can read your future here
If it's bleak, never fear!
We have just the charm for that —
Just ignore the undead rat.

When the moon falls from the sky
And you fear that you could die
Come to Sparky's Magic Shop
There's no problem we can't stop!

King of Clubs

Once he was a simple knave
with a talent for a tune,
whether lute or flute or song
he'd woo the girls under the moon.

One day a new maid, pale and mute,
he serenaded with words like magic;
she glowed and laughed with joy once more,
but that is where his tale turned tragic.

This maid was engaged to a brute
who with his sword sought revenge;
our hero left town to escape,
sought refuge in a hidden henge.

There he was found by roving troupe,
they read his fate within the cards:
his future safe from vengeful wrath
if he became their loyal bard.

Traveling from sea to sea,
he entranced patrons at the pubs;
evermore the ladies man,
earned the name the King of Clubs.

To Be a Hero?

A youth seeking guidance
kneels before the village matron.
She rests her withered hand
atop the boy's bowed head.

"We found you in the woods —
a babe crying alone.
You welcomed our embrace
and we gave you a home.

Now your eager hands
ask for a sword;
your restless feet
long to wander.

Dear child,
sometimes it's better not to question.
Knowledge may be power,
but the answers may distort your view.

If you pursue destiny
through the twilit forest,
you will leave inexperienced,
exposed to your rival's whim.

Take heed to your elder now.
Don't take that first step to see the wizard;
once that path is chosen, you cannot return.
Embrace the life you have —
leave the world to its own devices."

And the boy lifts his head
to see this village, his home,
wondering if his purpose
is greater than self,
and questions if fate is his to choose.

Door Three: The Fae Realm

Where beauty dazzles and danger dances close behind.

The door creaks open on golden hinges.
The air tastes sweet,
heavy with secrets and song.

In these wild realms,
the rules are not your own.
Glimmering courts,
whispering woods,
the laughter of beings
older than dreams —
step carefully.
And leave a trail to find your way home.

(If you wish to come back.)

Dawn

dew
drops drip
down willow leaves
deluge sleeping fairy forms
awaken

wind
whispers through
woodland trails
wings dance through air
flirting

fairies
flaunt colors
spark fire dust
find kindred spirits
mate

blossom
new growth
tender bud opens
reveals hidden forms
newborn

Druid Ring

within circle of stones
hooded figures link hands
feet bare to connect
to the earth

voices join in song
as the sun
touches the mountain

they witness the night
a bonfire lit to keep darkness at bay
until the sun's return

each member steps forward
casts off that which holds them back
burns it in the flames

death and rebirth
a new year begins
honor the cycle

Miraluna Lake

Three ghosts haunt the pier
of Miraluna Lake,
seen only as the sun
descends into the water.
Dark shadows rise from damp planks,
flowing to form
father, son, daughter;

lives stolen by the Mud–Monster,
our version of Loch Ness;
camouflaged in twilight,
coated in sludge,
feeding on the fishers,
creating a new link
in the food chain.

These three new spirits
dare not leave their post,
warning the unwary:
the calm waters
are merely a lie.

Spring's Firstborn

Light sneaks through
broken clouds,
mounds of snow glisten,
as snowflakes relax into water.

One mound shifts
to birth slender horn,
then narrow head.

The equine snorts fog —
lurches to her feet,
shakes off winter's remnants.

Her first whinny
wakes spring from its slumber.
She walks the thawing earth,
flowers blooming with each step,

Fairy Fudge

the fairies left a gift for me
outside my bedroom door —
a single square of darkest fudge
you won't find in a store.

pixie dust like little stars
glinting from its core,
it carries whiffs of oak
soaked in rain's downpour.

I take a bite and close my eyes,
relish tastes galore...
cocoa rivers carry me
to exotic shores.

magic bursting through my veins,
my feet lift off the floor —
wings curl from my shoulders
leaving muscles sore.

I shrink down to inches high,
needing clothes no more;
wrapped only in morning light...
out the door I soar.

Jackalope

The jackalope hops o'er the hills
aware as the hare
regal as the deer
it skirts the desert towns
rarely seen but sometimes heard
singing with its flaggerdoot
echoes woven from our songs
as thunder rolls above

Gnomish Noise

Skitter skitter
goes the house gnome
always heard yet never seen.

Creak creak
go the floor boards
while he tries to make them clean.

Pitter patter
past my door
finding lost things is his routine.

Humming humming
at the gift bowl
as he dines on fine cuisine.

A Series of Fairy Fine Limericks

There once was a girl from the sea,
To a little old man made a plea.
She traded her eggs
For a nice pair of legs —
Now her children will never be free.

There once was a red–hooded girl
Who through the dark woods did twirl,
'Til a sound made her scream
And fall in a stream —
Turned out it was only a squirrel.

There once was a girl from Cancun
Who couldn't carry a tune.
Her song for a meal
Made a werewolf reel —
And now she howls at the moon.

Masquerade

The fae came to my masquerade;
satyr, nymph, or mere human
free to mingle,
hooves and feet dance to same tune.

Costumes, masks, horns, wings,
who is to say what is real?
That fairy looks to shimmer
but it could just be the wine.

A tall, handsome wolf
offers his white gloved hand,
spins me on the dance floor,
whispers stories in my ear.

A night of music, magic, mystery.
By night's end I'm tipsy,
whether from spell or wine
I fear I will remember little,
when dawnlight breaks
the glamour of the night.

Changeling

They tricked Mother
You have to believe me
Skin prickles when he's hovering
He's not my little brother anymore
Eyes too wide and ever watching
Too keen for only five
Check him for horns

Rumpelstiltskin

He was a little man,
all sticks and bones,
who couldn't stand
a maiden's moans.

One day he heard
a young girl's cry;
poor girl was afraid
that she might die.

He asked of her
what he could do
to shut her up
and help her too.

Her horrid task
to him she told —
of all the straw
to make to gold.

She gave to him
her precious ring.
The job was done
before morning.

That night again
he heard her cry
(but not for lack
of lullaby).

The task had grown —
and thus the fee
this time he asked
for her baby.

The girl agreed
for she did know
unfinished work meant
her life would go.

The bargain was made,
the errand complete,
and in one year's time
the price she'd meet.

The baby came,
and then the man —
he simply took
the babe and ran.

But the mother's cries
once more did draw
him to her side;
her heart was raw.

He opened up
and to her gave
one last chance
her babe to save.

This time the cost
was guess his name
(he did not think
she'd win this game).

Two guesses he gave
to name him true.
She cried when she missed
the first of the two.

Her second guess
was way off course —
this time he left
with no remorse.

The child he took
to claim for his own,
leaving the mother
to cry alone.

So there is the story
of one little man
whose name, not guessed,
was Rumpelstiltskin.

Princess of the Waters

Some call them Children of Neptune,
mermaids, sirens of the sea
we three brothers
on our small fishing vessel
bestowed a name
on she

the first time
a splash
gone missing
a pocket watch
a shoelace

the next time
a flash of golden eyes
peering along water's surface
'neath twisted strands of hair

we tempted her
with baubles left on boat's edge
in return she teased us
with glimpses of ivory skin

a fortnight it took
to earn her trust
the moon a silver coin
glinting from the waters

new charm in hand
she pulled herself atop a rock
dripping hair and dark seaweed
clinging to curves

nimble fingers wove bracelet
into layers of hair
next to the watch chain
and a broken
seashell
tied with shoestring

musical trills greeted us
as our boat rowed nigh
dolphins came to join her song
'twas then we named her
Sabrina
princess of the waters

a sultry smile
a curl of finger
beckoned us to join her

our youngest brother did not hesitate
to slide into dark waters
lean on the rock beside her
she cupped his face
kissed him
mouths still joined she dove
taking him into the sea

so jealous were we
at the attention
the boat swayed as
we stood to join them
but the dolphins leapt
intercepting our every move

three now two
each night we return
yearning for another glimpse
bearing gifts in hope
for the prize of her kiss

each night in vain
she needs us no more
Sabrina has chosen her prince

Concrete Forest

Stench of pigeons
rouses me;
I uncurl from the nook
at the statue's collar,
flap my wings
to rid night's dust.

The birds share their crumbs —
pigeons and a fairy,
what a quaint family.

I fly low
in murky sky,
pollution heavy against my wings,
the touch of fresh air forgotten.

I perch on a windowsill,
peek in to watch the news:
humans fight yet flourish.
How did these self-destructive
beings displace
fairy kind?

A flower taken
from their make-believe garden —
small consolation
for the pain they bring —
bright petals held before me
I fly on.

I squeeze into the lighthouse —
now a dusty relic,
city's bright lights
leave no need for a beacon —
no one to offer
gifts of berries on the shelf
below rafters, once home;
now only my own
tiny footprints mar the dust.

Unwilling to disturb
the air with my wings
I tiptoe to their grave,
leave a tulip
on empty nest,
my tears cover it as dew.

No more berry feasts
and harvest dances,
no more clashing wings
and laughter.

I retreat,
limbs cold,
back into concrete forest
that replaced the wood so long ago.

Danse Macabre

She opens the envelope, crisp and formal,
flowing words invite her to the masquerade —
a gala so bizarre, near paranormal.

Her golden hair twisted in intricate braid,
she wears flowing white as pale as her face
and a butterfly mask of crimson suede.

At sunset she abandons her hiding place
to attend the ball, her dance so sublime
enchants the prince, who seeks her embrace.

They dance through the night, clock about to chime
moments before sunrise, she begs him to leave
yet he will not let go so she runs out of time.

The bells ring for dawn, her frightened gaze upturns
to sun's deadly rays as her vampire skin burns.

Fuel for the Myth

a burning home
a refined gem
smoldering passion
blacksmith's fire
mage's flame
orb of light
flickering candles
leading lamp

each fire a story,
forged in dream

Slumber

I stretch with the sun.
Too long have my limbs lain dormant.
The earth shifts, resists,
as I unroot my feet.
Clumsily, I step forward.
The spell of sleep still sings to me,
luring me back to rest.
If I do not move now, I shall ever remain —
Trapped in this hardened skin.

A voice calls on the wind,
cutting through the spell —
a chant to stir my bones.
I stumble to my knobby knees.
A hand reaches out to me.
My thin stick fingers take hers.

She is stronger than she seems,
her diaphanous form aglow in morning mist.
Pale hair whips across her face.
She will not let sloth
claim me again.

Leaves fall
as I shudder back to my feet.
Rough limbs shrink, lines fade.
With each step I become more like her —
skin smoothing,
moisture waking warmth in me.

The last dry foliage falls from my hair.
As my ankles break free
from the vines' confining grasp,
I run.

She smiles,
then disappears into the wind.
No longer seen,
but I feel her warmth inside,
pushing me forward.
My destiny awaits —
If only I do not let sloth take me.

Door Four: The Shadowed Realms

Where darkness holds both peril and possibility.

This door is heavy,
its wood scarred and worn.
It groans as it opens,
releasing a breath of chill air.

Beyond lies shadow,
where curses coil
and fears wear familiar faces.
There is something worth finding —
light,
flickering but fierce,
waiting for the one who dares to look.

Enter, if you are not afraid of the dark.

Hold Back the Horde

Alert the town, the enemy draws near;
The creatures feed by soaking in our fear.
Retreat into your homes 'til danger's past;
Calm now your children and we will outlast.

The demons circle, hunting as a pack.
Our rangers find high ground for the attack;
Let loose the arrows, let their mark be sure —
The demons' deaths our safety will ensure.

A single bowman steps into the fray;
A flame-tipped arrow readied for display.
With steady breath, he sparks the trail of oil
And sets their flesh to blister, burn, and boil.

The demons close, their talons rend his side.
The rangers charge and stem the surging tide,
Hold back the horde until the break of dawn;
The demons falter, haggard and withdrawn.

The victory is won but bittersweet,
The hero's wounds his ultimate defeat.
We plant new seeds where arrowheads once fell,
And sing of hope to hold the gates of hell.

Dark Days

She grips her sword, the battlefield looks stark,
Almost too late to set the world aright;
Hold ground, dig deep, the days are getting dark.

A flock of ravens circle through the park,
Abandoned structures gleaming in moonlight.
She grips her sword, the battlefield looks stark.

Filth clinging like a permanent birthmark,
Wendigo crouches just within her sight.
Hold ground, dig deep, the days are getting dark.

Her two companions circle like a shark —
Once enemies, they now combine their might —
She grips her sword, the battlefield looks stark.

The monster takes first blood: claws tear a mark
Through one man's side, his face goes deathly white.
Hold ground, dig deep, the days are getting dark.

Wendigo falters at a shotgun's bark
And blade moves in to finish off the fight.
She grips her sword, the battlefield looks stark;
Hold ground, dig deep, the days are getting dark.

Seasons by Clockwork

— Spring —
Mother fragile and sad,
no child can she bear;
Father, an inventor, makes me —
a clockwork child to be their son.
With a spring in step we walk
through the park together.

— Summer —
Mother brags of me —
Ladies join us for tea and cakes;
they marvel at my gears and form.
I run, dance, climb,
but when other youth go for a swim,
I am forbidden to join,
in fear of rust.

— Fall —
Foliage fades, so does Mother's health.
No more time for play;
I help with Mother's chores:
tending the garden,
cleaning house,
while other children go to school.

— Winter —
Now Mother has left us,
Father cannot bear to see me.
Those ladies, once intrigued,
don't want an unreal child.
Father has abandoned me;
left in the park we used to walk;
heart broken, I lay
half-covered in drifts of snow.

— Irrelevant —
Memories of Mother keep me here.
Seasons pass, rust and decay
chip away my shell
yet my heart ticks on
waiting, waiting, waiting
for someone to want me again.

Shadow's Heat

I rest in crevice shadow,
drift off into dream,
rushing me away from desert heat
to a hilltop drenched in rain,
where a dark coven stands amid stone —
performing an ancient ritual.

We abandon robes of shadow,
stand naked at the altar stone.
Rain cascades down my body,
leaves only a memory of arid heat.

One of the coven in the rain
clad only in cloud's gray shadow;
wondering now which part is dream,
desert shade or mountain stone.

Coven hands join
as altar flares in magic flame.
Lightning dances to banish shadow,
signals a pounding rain.

A shield forms to block the downpour —
invisible but firm as stone.
Within the fire a winged shadow,
eyes burn with ancient power.

My head pounds with the beating rain,
my body overtaken through ritual,
I fall to my knees before the stone —
flames expand to consume me in heat...
demon invades to dwell in my heart's shadow.

I wake from the dream, lying on desert stone,
yet still wet from rain and pulsing with magical heat,
branded by a ritual of darkest shadow.

Locked in Endless Darkness

I measure the myrrh,
sprinkle the liquid inside the sarcophagus.
Acolytes burn candles to fight off darkness.
A calf is brought and I remove its heart;
candlelight and shadow frame bloodied hands.

The chamber door bursts open,
blinding me with Ra's sun;
the floor trembles with an army of feet.
Shocked to see rival priests, I drop the heart;
it hits slanted floor and comes to rest
next to the one thing still in darkness —
the sarcophagus.

I lunge for the heart to finish the spell,
but the priests will not allow it;
they do not see shades between light and dark.
Their chants encase trembling limbs.
The spell burns with Ra's judgment:
Will it take me to eternal rest?

Their spell for a time stops my heart;
it beats once more as they lay my wrapped body
in the tomb.
Understanding dawns —
my punishment is worse than death's rest.
Linen over my eyes hides all but shifting shadows.

A scrape of coffin lid and all is dark;
all silent but for my beating heart.
Wrapped hands against the lid pound
but there is no escaping my tomb.
I beat until my body demands rest;

Hunger breaks me from my slumber;
here in the dark
terror grips my heart —
they completed the spells on the tomb.
Futility is all I see; despair my only companion.

My head pounds with the inability to rest;
After centuries entombed in the darkness,
My heart yearns for even a glimpse of Ra's light.

Once Upon a Mirror

This mirror made of witchery —
your image haloed in the glass,
I see you looking back at me.

Your lips quirked with subtle sass
I yearn to touch those trembling wings
Your image haloed in the glass.

My fingers press, the cold glass stings.
I must free the fae within,
I yearn to touch those trembling wings.

I focus will, and begin
murmur spells once overheard
I must free the fae within.

You add your whisper, echoed word —
I have lost control —
murmur spells once overheard

A flash, light fades, we have switched roles
This mirror made of witchery
I have lost control...

I see you looking back at me.

Werewolf

Wolf
full moon
howls echo
humanity
gone

Bite

Dark
shadows
in the night
vampires hiding
BITE!

The Reign of the Night

Two brothers stride through cold, relentless rain,
Our destination lost — we're going nowhere.
Afraid to face what we already know:
The lies we told ourselves would not hold true.
We wear them still, but they can't last the night,
When hunger's reign demands its fatal proof.

We find a barn, a refuge of no proof
Against the creeping hunger of the rain.
But danger waits, coiled silent in the night —
Tooth and claw tear us, leaving us nowhere
To run. My brother's cries are sharp and true;
We bleed. And in the dark, we come to know.

We die — and rise again. And now we know
Ourselves remade, though neither asked for proof.
My brother laughs, his joy both fierce and true,
While I resist the pulse that falls like rain.
He hunts at dusk, his conscience left nowhere,
While I still shun the terrors of the night.

A girl appears — a lamb in wolfish night.
My brother smiles. He's sure she'll never know
Until too late, and leaves her hope nowhere.
But I can hear the heartbeat, loud and true.
I hold myself in tight control, a rein
Of iron will against a need for proof.

My brother scoffs. He's done with games of proof.
He tells me to embrace this gifted night.
He speaks of power falling soft as rain,
Of secrets men and gods could never know.
He says we'll carve a kingdom, fierce and true,
And rule the dusk. There's nothing for us nowhere.

He leads, though once his heart led him nowhere.
He's found his purpose — now he'll prove it true.
I watch him take his place within the night,
And wonder at this brother I now know.
If I remain, I'll lose my iron rein
And fall into the dark to seek my proof.

We wander where the shadows birth the night.
I see his path and know it to be true.
Our thirst, the proof, descends in crimson rain.

Unrequited

Hidden in oak tree's shadow,
I lean forward...
gripping the branch with clawed feet.
He leaves the inn. Laughing,
a toss of burnished hair;
in excitement I almost lose my balance,
flap my wings to steady myself.
He looks up.
I pull back from his piercing green gaze,
burrow my head in my shoulder.
He must not see me.

His footsteps distance, and I
dare to peek again.
A pretty young thing leans
out a window to catch his eye;
I hiss at her, but his attention
already moved on —
to assist a woman into her carriage;
she is no beauty, wrinkled as I.
Breath rushes out in surprise.
Perhaps...

In my hesitation, I almost lose him.
Over rooftops I fly,
skittering across tiles
to perch on a ledge.
I crane to see but he enters a shop.
I yearn to follow, to speak to him,
but shudder at the sight he would see.

I retreat to my oak,
settle my crooked back into the hollow,
wrap my tattered filthy wings
around my ungainly breasts,
and dip my head, that my oily hair
covers my haggard visage.

How would a prince such as he
see past looks
to love this harpy?

Witch's Spell

A newborn Wisp
for vitality

A strand of web
for intrigue

Rose complete with thorns
for romance

A ribbon of silk
for attraction

A golden coin
for royalty

And then the new
Queen I shall be

Door Five: The Celestial Skies

Where dreams are written in starlight.

This door is made of silver mist.
It parts at your touch,
revealing endless sky.

Here, the stars sing.
Gods walk the horizon,
and wishes take flight
on wings of light and hope.

The stories told here
are older than time
and brighter than memory.
Look up.
The sky is waiting.

Secrets in the Stars

Stars twinkle in code...
a message from another universe.
If only I could decipher it,
what secrets would they share?

Perhaps they'd reveal
the formula for life,
or warn of an invasion.

It could be our wishes
sent out to the powers that be.

Or maybe it's nothing so grand —
just lonely stars
trading notes in the night,
like a student passing folded paper,
just pass it on.
And even if I took a peek,
it would have no meaning for me.

Charm of Night

I ask for sweet dreams
with the birth of this charm
flower of buckwheat
protects me from harm

feather of owl
to watch as I sleep
sprinkled with moondust
to make my dreams deep

amethyst stone
will calm the mind
then strips of willow
will this charm bind.

Courtship Song

Song 1 - of mortals

A tale I sing of girl meets boy
He labored in her pa's employ
With wooden flute he played a tune
They danced beneath the Courtship Moon

They walked and talked, their love grew swift
One day he shared a precious gift
A gold pendant to make her swoon,
They danced beneath the Courtship Moon

A picnic meal down by the lake
Where he proposed her hand to take
With hearts that yearned to marry soon
They danced beneath the Courtship Moon

Song 2 - of immortals

From out of darkness came a birth
And Moon looked down on Mother Earth
His heart engaged, he took a chance
As Earth and Moon resume their dance

With one full turn, from left to right
He courted her most every night
Then with a nod, they each advance
As Earth and Moon resume their dance

Their love makes magic with each breath
From birth, to marriage, then to death
An endless cycle of romance
As Earth and Moon resume their dance

Fate

Five doomed us...
A council of greed
turned to the dark arts
in their attempts to cheat death,
but only gods can grant immortality.

Foresight could have saved us...
the oracle's visions blinded by gold,
she bought a ship
and left us to our fates.

Thrice the waves came,
each more deadly than the last...
slammed through walls,
flooded streets,
pushed us to the heart of our island.

Too little, too late,
a sacrifice was chosen
to appease the scorned gods:
I was merely a child
thrown into the volcano's maw.

One last desperate prayer,
I cried out in terror
as I fell to certain doom:
this wasn't my fault,
wasn't my fate!

Zero hour had come...
Hades embraced me,
blessed my sacrifice;
I ascended as Atlantis crumbled,
reborn as a phoenix.

Fire Dragon

This cousin to salamanders,
conceived in Earth's molten core,
has coal black eyes
and power rippling under its scales.
Beware its searing breath.
This most majestic of creatures
spreads its crimson wings,
dominating the skies.

From Ashes

Earth burning, ashes
fill the sky until it rains —
ready for rebirth.

Lone egg bursts open;
red wings flutter in new air.
Phoenix is reborn

Ballad of Eleuteria

The Goddess of the Fey was She,
Only love could bind Her;
The same 'twill be that sets Her free
Once ruin doth occur.

A group of men set on a trip
To seek the fabled lass.
Getaf and Gii did wreck their ship,
The price for their trespass.

A storm did wash a man ashore
Her isle within the mist.
The ship He led would sail no more,
The crew did not exist.

'Twas new for Her to sympathize
Toward one of mankind.
She nursed Him to thwart His demise,
And found Their hearts entwined.

The Goddess of the Fey was She,
Only love could bind Her;
The same 'twill be that sets Her free
Once ruin doth occur.

As one They traveled o'er the land;
A child was soon conceived.
Their love so strong it would demand
More cost than They believed,

For Her lover was no mere man,
Enchanter blood had He.
Some feared Their union and began
To set their own decree:

They sought to take the Couple's life,
After the child was born.
And thus enchanters caused the strife
Which Fey have come to mourn.

The Goddess of the Fey was She,
Only love could bind Her;
The same 'twill be that sets Her free
Once ruin doth occur.

Caught unawares the Daughter died
Within a forest glade.
The Goddess wounded as She cried
So He came to Her aid.

He banished Her with one last spell,
His life exchanged for Hers —
Within the forest She would dwell
'Til one removed the curse:

Born of enchanter and of Fey,
You'll know her by this sign:
She'll hear the Goddess cry and say
"My sorrow is as Thine."

The Goddess of the Fey was She,
Only love could bind Her;
The same 'twill be that sets Her free
Once ruin doth occur.

She must leave all she knows behind,
Go where They once did meet.
Magic alone will not unbind
The spell of Her defeat.

Remember well this vital song,
For if the moment lost
The Goddess will be ever gone,
Her life the final cost.

Protect this forest area,
Do not forget this day.
Her name was Eleuteria,
His name was Monderay.

Moon's Song to Earth

Only you and I,
in our daily dance through stars,
can arouse the sun.

Each coming morning,
as your children rise to toil,
I rest in your arms.

If we don't persist —
as we have since time began —
our loyal cycle,

the sun would witness.
In the depths of its despair,
it may drench itself,

the light in the sky
and the magic in this world
snuffed out in sorrow.

Lullaby for a Star God

Rest, little Deo'Tu,
'neath fairy lights
wrapped in elven silk
rocking in a dwarven cradle
muses sing o'er you
dragons warm you with their breath
humans nurse you
downy hair of darkest night
silver skin reflects the light
eyes golden as the sun
many hearts will be won
son of stars
child of prophecy
all creatures praise your name

Door Six: The Storyteller's Door

Where you become the dreamer and the maker.

At the end of all journeys
stands this door —
quiet,
plain,
yet thrumming with possibility.

This is the doorway to creation,
where the ink of your heart
writes worlds into being.

You are the storyteller now.
Take up the quill.
What world will you make?

I Turn Away No More

I tried to leave you once,
But found myself an empty shell —
My soul starved without your voice
Whispering sweet tales into my mind.

When thoughts of you returned to me
I could not turn them away.
I thought that I created you,
But you're the one that feeds me life.

A fire burns within me,
As the stories swarm chaotically.
I give them full reign, as
You fill my soul once more.

Thus newly committed,
I sit and listen to your voice
As you tell your tale
And the words emerge on paper.

Ubduk

A grimy little troll
sneaks in when you take a break
and kidnaps Muse
when you need her most.

This anti-muse leaves only
a puddle of doubts,
like a carton of kittens
mewling for attention.

"You're not good enough."
"The market is saturated."
"Your ideas are boring."
"Too out there."
"You'll never be a serious Artist."
"Who would ever pay for this?"

Fierce whispers dig into
your heart until you embrace
them as truth.

By the time Muse
breaks free of Ubduk,
doubt has clawed
deep inside,
making it harder
to grasp
inspiration.

Flighty Muse

Keep your Muse close
charm her so she will not stray
play the music she prefers
humor her need to lead,
even if it takes you off your chosen path.

If perchance she disappears,
bar your door with friend's support
do not let Ubduk fill the empty space.

Read the works that you have written
remember why you write
find your passion
power attracts power
to call back Muse.

Keep writing to hold back doubts
be ready for her return
and she will come back to you.

The Author

A goddess, many worlds do I create
to fill with danger, passion, magic, flight,
with words alone manipulating fate.

A lonely princess on a grand estate,
a dragon in his lair just out of sight,
a goddess, many worlds do I create.

Each character is given a strong trait
then thrown into some unforgiving plight;
with words alone manipulating fate.

When countless suitors seek to procreate,
the dragon takes them out with just a bite.
A goddess, many worlds do I create.

A hero uses wit to then debate
and keeps the dragon occupied all night,
with words alone manipulating fate.

The dragon tricked to eat some poisoned bait —
the princess freed to her own tale rewrite.
A goddess, many worlds do I create,
with words alone manipulating fate.

A Fairy's Prize

Your journal, it drew my eye
each time I peeked in all shy.
Its spine is the same rich orange
of autumn and monarch butterflies.

Room empty one morning at dawn
I flit from the windowsill,
tiptoe across the desk —
loose papers flutter to the floor.

I push aside the notepad
sitting atop my prize —
gasp at the girl looking back
from the cover.

Surrounded by butterflies
and falling petals,
is a fairy just like me.

That discovery sealed its fate.
I whistle to my friends —
four pairs of hands and wings
to haul our treasure home.

Hidden between fences,
tucked within brambles,
our nest is a burst of color
between your world and mine.

Propped against a rock,
dust dances when I heave the cover open;
Wingtips brush as we all lean close...
drawn by the book's charm.

We gasp in awe as pages turn
at the album of our favorite things:
pictures of fairies, butterflies, sunsets,
plastered across the pages.

Poems that skip down the lines,
lyrics and quotes and lists.
The journal's mantra resonating
Smile, play, be free.

The last page, empty,
yearns for our mark...
giggling, we dip bare feet in berry juice
leave tiny prints from one side to the next.

Someday when we are done
with our joy and play
we shall return this book to you,
a gift of our magic left inside.

Fly with Me

Child, put your hand in mine and fly with me,
Fly with me.
Away from this harsh city fly with me,
Above the rooftops we will soar
Away from hunger and sadness.
Get high on the rising air,
Feel the addictive madness,
Fly with me.

Through dripping clouds, to clear sky, fly with me,
Fly with me.
Beneath distant gleaming stars, fly with me.
Once we're chilled from the thin crisp air
We'll soar with a hot desert breeze.
Exhausted we'll return home,
'Til you come back with your pleas,
"Fly with me."

Child, attend closely as you fly with me,
Fly with me,
To soar solo when you can't fly with me.
Then when my limbs forget to fly,
These memories faded and gray,
Come to my door and greet me,
Take my withered hand and say,
"Fly with me."

I believe

I believe
in you, in me,
that fantasy can be reality.

I can change the world,
not by being big, but being myself.
I can make a difference
one person at a time.

I will change someone's world,
and that means the world to me.

There is magic in this world.
I want to share that magic with you.
Will you share your world with me?

Beyond the Threshold

The doors are open now,
And you hold the key;
Go —
Enchantment awaits.
Your own story begins.

Acknowledgements

Thank you to my beta readers for reading through these poems and collections so many times. Your input was invaluable.

Thank you to the editors of the following publications where earlier versions of some poems in this collection first appeared:

"Dark Days" in *Local Gems Poetry Press.*
"Changeling" in *Abyss & Apex.*
"Princess of the Waters" in *Moon Drenched Fables* and later in *Lifelines,* a collection by my poetry group The Poetic Muselings.

Earlier versions of the following poems were published in my debut collection, Chiaroscuro:

"Shadow's Heat," "Princess of the Waters," "Miraluna Lake" (as "Mirramisu Lake"), "Changeling," "Ubduk," "Defending the Keep," "Danse Macabre," "Concrete Forest," and "Dark Days."

About the author

Mary W. Jensen lives in Utah with her husband and son. Mary is the middle of nine children, and escaped the loudness of reality by immersing herself in books and poetry. From chaos comes creation. She is the author of the Tales of Tessagonia series, fairytale novellas set in a shared world, and the poetry book *Chiaroscuro*. Her poetry has been published in the webzines *Moon Drenched Fables*, *Abyss & Apex*, and *Snapdragon Journal*. She is also co-author of the poetry book *Lifelines* by The Poetic Muselings.

You can find Mary online at BriarbookLane.com.

Also by Mary W. Jensen

Tales of Tessagonia Series

The Blazing Princess

Mirror

The Princess Test

Venom and Shadow

The Gloaming Realm

The Moon Prince

Jack and the Midnight Cloak

The Drowned Song

Poetry

Chiaroscuro

Doorways to Enchantment

9 781737 643722